Beware the Jabberwock

by Ron Nicol

Single copies of plays are sold for reading purposes only. The copying or duplicating of a play, or any part of play, by hand or by any other process, is an infringement of the copyright. Such infringement will be vigorously prosecuted.

Baker's Plays
7611 Sunset Blvd.
Los Angeles, CA 90042
BAKERSPLAYS.COM

NOTICE

This book is offered for sale at the price quoted only on the understanding that, if any additional copies of the whole or any part are necessary for its production, such additional copies will be purchased. The attention of all purchasers is directed to the following: this work is fully protected under the copyright laws of the United States of America, the British Commonwealth, including Canada, and all other countries of the Copyright Union. Violations of the Copyright Law are punishable by fine or imprisonment, or both. The copying or duplication of this work or any part of this work, by hand or by any process, is an infringement of the copyright and will be vigorously prosecuted.

This play may not be produced by amateurs or professionals for public or private performance without first submitting application for performing rights. Royalties are due on all performances whether for charity or gain, or whether admission is charged or not. Since performance of this play without the payment of the royalty fee renders anybody participating liable to severe penalties imposed by the law, anybody acting in this play should be sure, before doing so, that the royalty fee has been paid. Professional rights, reading rights, radio broadcasting, television and all mechanical rights, etc. are strictly reserved. Application for performing rights should be made directly to BAKER'S PLAYS.

No one shall commit or authorize any act or omission by which the copyright of, or the right to copyright, this play may be impaired. No one shall make any changes in this play for the purpose of production.

Publication of this play does not imply availability for performance. Both amateurs and professionals considering a production are strongly advised in their own interest to apply to Baker's Plays for written permission before starting rehearsals, advertising, or booking a theatre.

Whenever the play is produced, the author's name must be carried in all publicity, advertising and programs. Also, the following notice must appear on all printed programs, "Produced by special arrangement with Baker's Plays."

Licensing fees for BEWARE THE JABBERWOCK is based on a per performance rate and payable one week in advance of the production.

Please consult the Baker's Plays website at www.bakersplays.com or our current print catalogue for up to date licensing fee information.

Copyright © 2009 by Ron Nicol
Made in U.S.A.
All rights reserved.

BEWARE THE JABBERWOCK
ISBN **978-0-87440-215-5**
1895-B

BEWARE THE JABBERWOCK was suggested by the poem 'Jabberwocky' in Lewis Carroll's *Through the Looking Glass*. The play can be performed by young people alone, or by combined youth and adult groups of all sizes. The text suggests that there are 3 Toves, 2 Borogroves and 2 Raths, but there is scope for additional non-speaking creatures of each kind, and lines may be re-allocated to provide something for extra characters to say. Some doubling of roles might also be possible. Although 'he' and 'she' have been used throughout, most creatures can be male or female, with the pronoun changed appropriately.

BEWARE THE JABBERWOCK was shortlisted in the Youth Section of the Drama Association of Wales One Act playwriting competition 2006 and in the Youth Section of the Scottish Community Drama Association Play on Words One Act playwriting competition 2006. The play, directed by Norma Nicol, was first produced by Glenrothes Theatre Company's Junior Players in June 2007 with the following cast:

EMMA	Mahri Smith
LUCY	Bethan Massie
FIRST TOVE	Erryn Miller
SECOND TOVE	Stacey Miller
THIRD TOVE	Shannon McCabe
JUBJUB BIRD	Amanda Wallace
QUEEN	Chelbie McMahon
FIRST BOROGROVE	Aine Pocock
SECOND BOROGROVE	Alan McGee
FIRST RATH	Jodie McGee
SECOND RATH	Jack Sweeney
PRINCE PERCY	Matthew Bain
TUMTUM TREE	Aine Pocock
JABBERWOCK	Steven Bain
FIRST BANDERSNATCH	Eilidh Smith
SECOND BANDERSNATCH	Caitlin Massie

CHARACTERS

EMMA
LUCY, HER YOUNGER SISTER
FIRST TOVE
SECOND TOVE
THIRD TOVE
JUBJUB BIRD
THE QUEEN
FIRST BOROGROVE
SECOND BOROGROVE
FIRST RATH
SECOND RATH
PRINCE PERCY
TUMTUM TREE
JABBERWOCK
FIRST BANDERSNATCH
SECOND BANDERSNATCH

PLACE

Tulgey Wood

TIME

Storytime

For Joe, Jamie, Otto and Orin.

*(**SETTING**: A sunny glade in a wood, surrounded by bushes. There's a sundial upstage center, several signs reading 'To Tulgey Wood' each pointing in a different direction, a small sign 'Keep Off The Grass' and a large one 'Beware the Jabberwock'.)*

*(**EMMA** and **LUCY** are sitting on the ground. **EMMA** is reading "Jabberwocky," but **LUCY** has fallen asleep with her head resting in **EMMA**'s lap.)*

EMMA. *(reading)* 'Beware the Jabberwock, my son! The jaws that bite, the claws that catch! Beware the Jubjub bird, and shun the frumious Bandersnatch!'

(looks down)

Oh. Lucy, you've fallen asleep! You can't think much of my reading, that's clear.

*(strokes **LUCY**'s hair)*

Mind you, I'm feeling rather tired myself…

*(**EMMA** yawns, and soon falls asleep. A head pops out from behind a tree or a bush, peers about and pops back. Another head pops out somewhere else, peers about, and pops back. Then a third. Soon heads are popping out and in everywhere – the more the better. A weird creature emerges cautiously. The **FIRST TOVE**. It looks carefully all round. Several other **TOVES** cautiously appear. The **SECOND TOVE** checks the sundial.)*

SECOND TOVE. Brillig!

FIRST TOVE. Is it?

SECOND TOVE. Of course it is. The sundial says so, and the sun's never wrong.

THIRD TOVE. Time to gyre.

FIRST TOVE. Time to gimble!

SECOND TOVE. It is, isn't it!

THIRD TOVE. You can say that again!

SECOND TOVE. It is, isn't it!

THIRD TOVE. You just had to do that, didn't you? Just had to say it again.

SECOND TOVE. You expected me to. It's a joke.

THIRD TOVE. I'm not very good at jokes.

FIRST TOVE. Stop gribing, you two! The sun's out! Come on, Toves, let's gyre and gimble!

THIRD TOVE. Wait! There's somebody here.

*(The **TOVES** gather round **EMMA** and **LUCY**. The **FIRST TOVE** reaches out cautiously and gently pushes **EMMA**, who stirs but doesn't wake. The **SECOND TOVE** prods **LUCY**, who wakes and sits up. **LUCY** and the **TOVES** stare at each other for a moment or two until the **TOVES** quickly exit wherever possible. **LUCY** shakes **EMMA**, who wakes.)*

LUCY. Emma! I saw something. They looked like badgers, but I don't think they were.

EMMA. You imagined it. It's that poem about slithy toves gyring and gimbling in the wabe…

LUCY. And the mome raths and borogroves. I remember.

EMMA. Come on, it's getting late and we ought to go home. It's this way, I think…

*(**EMMA** and **LUCY** exit. The **TOVES** peep out cautiously from their hiding places. **EMMA** and **LUCY** re-enter. The **TOVES** withdraw.)*

LUCY. This is where we started.

EMMA. Oh. Well – maybe it's this way…

*(They exit. The birds have stopped singing. The **TOVES** peep out cautiously from their hiding places then withdraw as **EMMA** and **LUCY** re-enter.)*

LUCY. It's the very same place again. Come on, Em, own up. We're lost, aren't we?

EMMA. Everything's changed somehow, and these signs are all pointing in different directions. And we don't want to go to Tulgey Wood – we're already in it and we want to get out of it.

LUCY. *(reading the sign)* 'Beware the Jabberwock'. Why do we have to beware the Jabberwock?

EMMA. I think it means 'beware *of* the Jabberwock'.

LUCY. I know that, silly, but why should we beware? Oh. That's the one in the poem, isn't it? With jaws that bite and claws that catch? Or is that the Jubjub Bird?

JUBJUB BIRD. *(off)* Jubjub! Jubjub! Jubjub!

(The light dims as a dark shadow crosses upstage from right to left. The **JUBJUB BIRD***.)*

LUCY. Oh, look! What a strange bird. Couldn't we…?

EMMA. No we couldn't! The creatures in this wood might be dangerous.

LUCY. Beware the Jabberwock!

EMMA. No, Lucy. The Jabberwock doesn't really exist –

LUCY. Then why's this sign here?

(A small round **QUEEN** *enters right. She's out of breath and looking very worried.)*

QUEEN. Oh our goodness! Oh, our beard and whiskers!

(While **EMMA***'s attention is on the* **QUEEN***,* **LUCY** *exits unobtrusively upstage left.)*

EMMA. Excuse me, could you help us?

QUEEN. Awfully sorry, can't stop. Busy, busy. Oh, our beard and whiskers!

(The **QUEEN** *rushes across the stage and exits left.)*

EMMA. Wait! Oh, she's gone. We'd better go too. Lucy! Where are you? Oh no, the silly girl must've gone after that bird.

*(***EMMA** *exits left. The* **TOVES** *enter.)*

FIRST TOVE. They've gone. We can gyre and gimble in peace…

(The **BOROGROVES** *enter right.)*

FIRST BOROGROVE. Right then, you Toves, move on. No gyring and gimbling here. The wabe is ours.

FIRST TOVE. No it isn't.

SECOND TOVE. *(raising its fists)* We'll fight you for it.

FIRST BOROGROVE. We refuse to stoop to fisticuffs to defend what's undeniably our own property.

SECOND TOVE. *(dancing about with fists raised)* Come on! Put up your hands.

SECOND BOROGROVE. We don't have hands.

FIRST TOVE. Scared, eh?

SECOND BOROGROVE. Yes – I mean, no, of course not.

SECOND TOVE. *(dancing about belligerently)* Put 'em up, put 'em up! Come on, put em up!

SECOND BOROGROVE. Now look here…

> *(As the* **SECOND BOROGROVE** *steps forward, the* **SECOND TOVE** *takes fright and dodges behind one of the others.)*

THIRD TOVE. Look out! They're coming back! They're coming back!

> *(The* **TOVES** *disappear as* **EMMA** *enters left.)*

EMMA. Lucy? Is that you? Oh!

FIRST BOROGROVE. Can't you read the signs, young lady? Keep off the grass.

EMMA. But there's grass everywhere. I can't help walking on it.

FIRST BOROGROVE. Just because you can't doesn't mean you wouldn't if you could, so you should even if you can't.

EMMA. I beg your pardon?

FIRST BOROGROVE. You can beg my pardon all you like, but I'm not going to argue legalities and technicalities with an inferior creature like you.

EMMA. Inferior creature!

FIRST BOROGROVE. Do you deny you're an inferior creature?

EMMA. I should think I do!

FIRST BOROGROVE. You only think so? Don't you know?

EMMA. Of course I do!

FIRST BOROGROVE. You might think you know, you might even know you think, but you obviously can't read because the sign says 'Keep Off The Grass.' And don't stare. It's rude to stare.

EMMA. You're staring at me. Aren't you being rude?

FIRST BOROGROVE. I could be much ruder than this if I tried.

EMMA. Please don't, you're quite rude enough as it is. Who are you, anyway?

FIRST BOROGROVE. We're The Borogroves. I expect you've heard of us.

EMMA. Of course. I'm pleased to meet you, Mr Borogrove – or is it Mrs Borogrove?

FIRST BOROGROVE. *The* Borogroves. Don't you know what '*The*' means? *The* Borogroves. The *original* Borogroves.

EMMA. *(holding out her hand)* Pleased to meet you.

FIRST BOROGROVE. Don't come too close! Who knows what diseases you might be carrying. And there are fleas, of course.

EMMA. I don't have fleas.

FIRST BOROGROVE. Maybe you do and maybe you don't –

EMMA. I don't!

FIRST BOROGROVE. Don't interrupt! Know your place, young lady, and mind your tongue!

EMMA. Well I never!

FIRST BOROGROVE. I'm not surprised you haven't, if that's your attitude.

(The **FIRST BOROGROVE** *turns its back and sulks.)*

SECOND BOROGROVE. Please don't take offence. I'm delighted to make your acquaintance.

EMMA. *(holding out her hand)* Pleased to meet you. Oh – you don't have hands…

SECOND BOROGROVE. No matter. Bowing is a much superior method of greeting.

(The **SECOND BOROGROVE** *bows.* **EMMA** *returns the bow. The* **SECOND BOROGROVE** *bows again.* **EMMA** *starts to bow in return but then realises that these formalities could go on for ever.)*

EMMA. I wonder, have you seen my little sister Lucy anywhere? I've lost her.

SECOND BOROGROVE. How very careless. Have you enquired at the Lost Property Office?

EMMA. No, I haven't. Where is it?

SECOND BOROGROVE. Nobody's seen it for ages, but as your sister's Lost Property, that's where you should enquire.

EMMA. But I don't know where to find it.

SECOND BOROGROVE. If you knew where to find it, it wouldn't be the *Lost* Property Office, would it?

EMMA. *(exasperated)* But that doesn't make sense!

SECOND BOROGROVE. Nothing makes sense in Tulgey Wood. It's much more fun that way. You'll get used to it.

EMMA. I don't want to get used to it. I want to go home – as soon as I've found my sister. I wonder if you'd mind telling me where I am?

SECOND BOROGROVE. Well, this is the exact centre of the wood. It's called the wabe.

EMMA. The wabe? Why?

SECOND BOROGROVE. Because it stretches way before us, and way behind us, and way beyond us in every direction, of course. Just follow the signs and when you can't see them any more you'll know you're out of the wood.

EMMA. But they all point in different directions. Which path should I take?

(The **FIRST BOROGROVE** *has had enough of sulking and decides to intervene.)*

FIRST BOROGROVE. My dear child! You can't take any of them. They don't belong to you!

EMMA. I mean, where does this path go?

FIRST BOROGROVE. It doesn't go anywhere. It has to stay where it is.

EMMA. But would it take me home?

FIRST BOROGROVE. If it were to take you home, what would people walk on till it came back?

EMMA. Oh dear, it seems one must be so careful with words.

FIRST BOROGROVE. Of course. Words and pathways are very alike. Each has its own appointed place, and if you confuse the poor thing it won't know where it belongs. It all depends what you want it to do.

SECOND BOROGROVE. If you ask it properly, this path could tell you how to get out of Tulgey Wood, it could tell you how to get home, or it might even tell you how to get into the middle of next week.

EMMA. But how does it tell me which is which?

SECOND BOROGROVE. It can't. It doesn't speak. That's what the signs are for.

FIRST BOROGROVE. I do wish you'd stop asking awkward questions, child. The only sensible questions are the ones to which you already know the answers.

EMMA. I wish my teacher knew that. She's always asking me questions when I don't know the answer.

FIRST BOROGROVE. Don't take any notice of teachers. They haven't any thoughts of their own – they simply follow the syllabus. It's one of the most annoying creatures in existence, the syllabus. It's always getting in the way and asking for attention. Just like you, in fact.

EMMA. Well!

FIRST BOROGROVE. I've had enough of this tedious conversation. I'm bored. We'll leave you and resume our perambulation through the wood.

SECOND BOROGROVE. If you're going to be hereabouts or thereabouts or anywhereabouts, beware the Jabberwock.

EMMA. I will. And the Jubjub Bird.

JUBJUB BIRD. *(off)* Jubjub! Jubjub! Jubjub!

SECOND BOROGROVE. It's not a good idea to mention the Jub – that bird. It listens at keyholes, you see, and when you say its name it comes looking for you. We ought to go, before it finds us.

(The light fades dramatically and the **BOROGROVES** *shuffle off hastily right as the* **JUBJUB BIRD** *enters left and chases after them.* **EMMA** *dodges to one side.)*

EMMA. It didn't see me. Oh my goodness, I do hope it didn't get Lucy!

(The **FIRST BANDERSNATCH** *peers onstage upstage left, makes beckoning gestures towards* **EMMA,** *and then withdraws.)*

EMMA. What on earth was that? I'd better find Lucy before something nasty finds her!

*(EMMA *exits left. The* **TOVES** *enter from various directions.)*

FIRST TOVE. Right! Time to gyre and gimble.

SECOND TOVE. Wait! There's somebody coming!

THIRD TOVE. Botheration!

(The **TOVES** *exit quickly as* **LUCY** *enters from right.)*

LUCY. Emma! Emma! Where are you?

(There's a small sad bellowing whistling sneezing sort of sound off-stage.)

FIRST RATH. *(off)* Oooooh – aaaah – weeee – choooh!

LUCY. What's that?

SECOND RATH. *(off)* Oooooh – aaaah – weeee – choooh!

LUCY. Well, it's not a frightening noise. It's a very small very scared creature sort of noise. Come out, come out, whoever you are. Don't be afraid. I won't hurt you.

(Two frightened **RATHS** *come out from behind the bushes.)*

FIRST RATH. Are you sure you won't hurt us?

LUCY. Of course I won't. I'm as scared as you are.

SECOND RATH. *(amazed)* Are you really? Truly? Absotootly scared?

LUCY. Absolutely.

SECOND RATH. Wow! Nobody's ever been scared of us before. We're usually the ones who get scareded.

LUCY. Well, you certainly scareded me. But I'm not scared now.

SECOND RATH. *(disappointed)* Not even a teeny weeny little bit?

FIRST RATH. *(severely)* We don't scare people.

SECOND RATH. I don't mind scaring people. It's fun!

FIRST RATH. *(firmly)* We don't scare people.

SECOND RATH. *(regretfully.)* If you say so. I just thought –

FIRST RATH. Don't. You know thinking isn't good for you. You get strange ideas when you think, and where would we be if they came true?

SECOND RATH. *(grumpily)* Still in the middle of Tulgey Wood, probabubbly.

LUCY. I'm looking for my big sister.

SECOND RATH. *(scared)* Oooh! Oooh! Ooh! How big is she? As big as a tree? As big as a heffalump?

LUCY. Just a little bit bigger than me.

SECOND RATH. Oh. That's all right then.

LUCY. She's called Emma. Have you seen her by any chance?

FIRST RATH. We haven't seen an Emma anywhere. Not anyhow.

SECOND RATH. Not nowhere. Not nohow. Absotootly.

RATHS. *(in unison)* Oooooh – aaaah – weeee – choooh!

SECOND RATH. *(jumps in fright)* Oooh! Oooh! Ooh! What was that?

FIRST RATH. That was us. Sneezing.

SECOND RATH. Oh. That's all right then.

LUCY. You must be the Raths. My sister's just been reading about you.

SECOND RATH. Reading about *us*? Really? Truly? Wow! We're famous!

FIRST RATH. We're not famous. Not really.

SECOND RATH. *(rebelliously)* I can pretend, can't I?

FIRST RATH. No you can't. It's like thinking, and I've told you about that before.

LUCY. I wonder, could you help me find my way out of the wood?

FIRST RATH. I'm afraid we can't. We're mome!

SECOND RATH. *(sadly)* Far from.

LUCY. Mome? Far from? Mome – far from – mome. Far from – far from home! Well, dear Raths, I'm far from mome as well, so we can look for it together. I must find Emma, and I'd like some company. I'm feeling rather lost and lonely myself.

(The **SECOND BANDERSNATCH** *peers on-stage upstage right and beckons, but as they turn it withdraws.)*

SECOND RATH. Oooh! Oooh! Ooh!

LUCY. What was that?

FIRST RATH. It's better not to ask! Come on, we'd better go this way.

(They exit left. As they pass, The **FIRST BANDERSNATCH** *reaches out and grabs at them with its long fingers, but misses. They don't notice and the* **FIRST BANDERS-NATCH** *tiptoes after them. The* **TOVES** *enter.)*

FIRST TOVE. Quickly, the sun's going down.

SECOND TOVE. Somebody's coming. Again!

THIRD TOVE. Botheration! Again!

(They exit in annoyance as the **QUEEN** *enters right, followed by* **EMMA.** *)*

EMMA. Please wait. Please! Only for a moment. I'm looking for my sister.

QUEEN. We're looking for our son. Have you seen him? Have you? He's a Prince, you know.

EMMA. Is he tall and handsome, dressed in silver armour and riding a white horse? Princes in story books always look like that.

QUEEN. Afraid not. Rather shabby. Dirty knees. Loud voice. Calls himself Sir Percival Lancelot Prancington Smythe. Really Prince Percy. Actually *is* a knight, you know. Passed the Knight School exams in spite of not being very clever. Mind you, most knights aren't very clever. Great disappointment to his father. Warned him. 'Beware the Jabberwock, my son!' he said. Now he's lost in the wood.

EMMA. My sister's called Lucy. She's lost too.

QUEEN. We'll look for them together, child. Four eyes are better than two, we always say, but four eyes are in such short supply nowadays. Have you noticed? But enough of this chattering and prattling. Must find our Percy! Come along child. Tallyho!

(They exit left. The **TOVES** *appear.)*

FIRST TOVE. This is most annoying. People walking all over the wabe like this.

SECOND TOVE. It shouldn't be allowed.

THIRD TOVE. Ssssh! They're coming back.

ALL TOVES. Botheration!

(The **TOVES** *exit as* **LUCY** *and the two* **RATHS** *enter right. The* **SECOND BANDERSNATCH** *reaches out upstage right and grabs at the rearmost* **RATH,** *but misses and withdraws unnoticed.)*

SECOND RATH. Excuse me. Would you mind walking a little slower? Your legs are so long, you see, and ours are so short.

FIRST RATH. Actually, if you don't mind, I think we'd rather go on by ourselves. It's what we do, you see. 'Rath' is a bit like 'rather' – we'd *rather* be on our own. If we found our way home, we wouldn't be lost any more, and then where would we be?

SECOND RATH. *(grumpily)* Still in the middle of Tulgey Wood, probabubbly.

RATHS. *(in unison)* Oooooh – aaaah – weeee – choooh!

SECOND RATH. Oooh! Oooh! Ooh! What's that?

FIRST RATH. It's just us. Sneezing. I've told you about that before.

SECOND RATH. Oh. That's all right, then.

LUCY. Maybe if you tried to be a little more cheerful, you wouldn't be so sad.

SECOND RATH. We don't mind being sad. We quite like it, really. Truly. Absotootly.

LUCY. 'Mome Raths outgrabe.' Is that what outgrabe means? That you're always sad?

FIRST RATH. It might, but it might not. It might mean we're glad to be sad. It might mean we're sad when we're glad. But then again, it might mean nothing at all. That's usually the case.

SECOND RATH. Oooh! Oooh! Ooh! Something's creeping up behind me! What is it? What is it?

FIRST RATH. It's just your shadow. I've told you about that before.

SECOND RATH. Oh. That's all right, then.

FIRST RATH. We must go. I do hope you find your sister. Beware the Jabberwock, won't you? The jaws and claws and things. Goodbye. It's this way, I think…

*(The **RATHS** exit left. The **SECOND BANDERSNATCH** enters from upstage right and tiptoes after the **RATHS**. **LUCY** doesn't notice.)*

LUCY. Why does everybody tell me to beware the Jabberwock? And what about the Jubjub Bird?

*(**LUCY** studies the signs, and the light fades dramatically as the **JUBJUB BIRD** enters upstage behind her, stealthily moving closer. It's about to tickle her with its long beak but at the last moment **LUCY** turns, sees the **JUBJUB BIRD** and backs away. The **JUBJUB BIRD** advances threateningly. **PERCY** enters with his sword drawn.)*

PERCY. Stand back, fair damson! I'll protect you! Have at thee, evil bird!

(**PERCY** *lunges at the* **JUBJUB BIRD** *with his sword.*)

JUBJUB BIRD. Jubjub! Jubjub! Jubjub!

PERCY. Gadzooks and Oddsboddikins! Defend thyself!

(Normal lighting is gradually restored as **PERCY** *fights the* **JUBJUB BIRD***, which uses its long beak as a sword.* **PERCY** *confuses the* **JUBJUB BIRD** *with dazzling swordplay consisting of extravagant twirls and flourishes of his blade – but without ever actually making contact with anything. Eventually the* **JUBJUB BIRD** *shrugs, gives up and exits.)*

LUCY. *(clapping enthusiastically)* That was marvellous. You were very brave.

PERCY. Was I? Was I really? Good of you to say so. I thought so too.

(bows)

Sir Percival Lancelot Prancington Smythe at your service.

LUCY. Thank you. I don't know what I'd have done if you hadn't rescued me.

PERCY. That's all right. It's what knights do. Rescue sore damsons in fair distress. I mean, fair damsons in sore distress. Or is it damsels? I'm never quite sure. Damsons, I think.

LUCY. I don't mind being a damson. I quite like damsons. But I can't call you Sir Percival Lancelot Prancington Smythe all the time. I'm going to call you Percy, for short.

PERCY. I'm not short! Mother says I'm quite tall for my age.

LUCY. Percy's a short way of saying Percival.

PERCY. Oh. I see.

(He obviously doesn't.)

You must be clever. I'm not clever at all.

LUCY. I'm not clever either, because I've managed to lose my sister. Could you help me?

PERCY. Well – I'm rather busy at the moment, I'm afraid. I'm on a perilous quest, you understand. You haven't seen the Jabberwock on your travels, by any chance?

LUCY. No, but I've seen a strange beckoning sort of creature…

(*The* **FIRST BANDERSNATCH** *peers onstage upstage left, beckons, and withdraws.*)

PERCY. No, that's not it. The Jabberwock whiffles through the wood and burbles as it comes.

JABBERWOCK. (*off*) Burble, burble. Burble, burble. Burble, burble.

PERCY. The very sound! I must make plans! Don't disturb me, I'm having uffish thoughts.

LUCY. Uffish? What's that?

PERCY. It means I'm feeling toughish, so my manner's roughish, my temper's huffish, and my voice is gruffish.

LUCY. 'So rested he by the Tumtum tree, and stood awhile in thought', that's what the poem says. You don't suppose there's a Tumtum tree anywhere about, do you?

(*A very short very round tree enters. The* **TUMTUM TREE.**)

TUMTUM TREE. Did somebody mention my name?

LUCY. Well, I mentioned it, but only in passing.

TUMTUM TREE. That's all right then. I'm only passing. Tum tum.

(*The* **TUMTUM TREE** *exits.*)

JABBERWOCK. (*off, nearer*) Burble, burble. Burble, burble. Burble, burble.

PERCY. The Jabberwock! I must pursue my perilous quest with all diligence. I must take my vorpal blade in hand, track down my manxsome foe and cut off its head. You can watch if you like.

(*He exits left, followed by* **LUCY.** *The* **TOVES** *enter – but merely shrug in resignation and exit again as* **EMMA** *and the* **QUEEN** *enter right.*)

EMMA. You know, it's very odd. No matter how far we walk, we always end up in the same place.

QUEEN. Of course, child. What else would you expect?

EMMA. I'd expect to get somewhere different.

QUEEN. That would never do. Much safer to end up in the same place. Never expect the unexpected, child. Makes life so unpredictable.

EMMA. I'm not going any further. I'm sure Lucy will find me if I stay here.

QUEEN. Of course she will, but where's the excitement in that? Much more fun to continue the search. Onwards, onwards, ever onwards! My old school motto, you know. Percy! Here boy! Come to your mother, Percy!

(The QUEEN *exits left. The lights begin a fast fade.)*

EMMA. Everybody round here is most contradictory! Oh my goodness, it's getting dark again.

JABBERWOCK. *(off, very near)* Burble, burble. Burble, burble. Burble, burble.

(The JABBERWOCK *enters upstage center. Its eyes gleam in the near darkness. It stands and sniffs the air.* EMMA *retreats left. The* JABBERWOCK *senses her presence and moves towards her. Suddenly* LUCY *enters right behind the* JABBERWOCK.*)*

LUCY. Leave my sister alone!

(The JABBERWOCK *turns right towards* LUCY. EMMA *jumps forward behind it.)*

EMMA. No! Over here!

(The JABBERWOCK *turns left towards* EMMA. PERCY *enters upstage behind the* JABBERWOCK.)*

PERCY. On guard, foul creature!

JABBERWOCK. *(startled, turning on* PERCY*)* Aaaah!

PERCY. *(equally startled)* Aaaah!

(The light slowly increases as PERCY *and the* JABBER-WOCK *circle each other cautiously,* PERCY *swinging his sword valiantly while the* JABBERWOCK *waves its claws. Neither is really sure what to do next.)*

PERCY. Keep still! How can I get at you if you keep dancing about?

JABBERWOCK. If I stand still, you'll hit me.

PERCY. That's the general idea. Gadzooks and Oddsboddikins! Have at thee!

(**PERCY** *indulges in some dazzling footwork and intricate swings with his sword without endangering the* **JABBERWOCK,** *who simply folds his arms and stands watching, tapping his foot impatiently. They're about to start circling again when* **LUCY** *steps between the combatants.*)

LUCY. Stop it!

PERCY. Never! I must o'ercome this loathsome creature or die in the attempt!

(**EMMA** *stands back to back with* **LUCY,** *keeping* **PERCY** *and the* **JABBERWOCK** *apart.*)

EMMA. Oh, come on. You've been playing around for ages.

PERCY. Playing around! These are some of my best moves, I'll have you know.

LUCY. It's perfectly obvious neither of you has any intention of hurting the other, so why don't you just shake hands and make up.

PERCY. *(waving his sword)* Never! I'm going to cut off his head!

JABBERWOCK. *(waving his claws)* Beware the jaws that bite, the claws that catch!

EMMA. Oh, do stop. You're giving me a headache.

PERCY. I'll stop if he stops.

JABBERWOCK. You stop first. Put down your sword.

PERCY. If you put down your claws.

LUCY. Don't be silly. How can he put down his claws?

PERCY. Well. Stop waving them about, then.

JABBERWOCK. If you stop waving your sword.

EMMA. This is ridiculous. I'll count to three, all right? Ready? One. Two. Three.

(**PERCY** *sheathes his sword. The* **JABBERWOCK** *puts his hands behind his back.*)

PERCY. We'll say I won.

JABBERWOCK. No, we won't.

PERCY. Why not?

JABBERWOCK. Because you didn't.

PERCY. I did!

JABBERWOCK. Didn't.

EMMA. For goodness sake! Will you two please stop!

LUCY. Why don't you call it a draw?

JABBERWOCK. Oh, all right, it's a draw. Agreed?

PERCY. Agreed. Sir Percy Lancelot Prancington Smythe, at your service. Who are you?

JABBERWOCK. Jim.

PERCY. I beg your pardon?

LUCY. Just Jim?

JABBERWOCK. Just Jim, I'm afraid. But I quite like being called the Jabberwock. They call me that because I talk too much, you see, but I don't get much chance to talk because everybody thinks I'm a ferocious creature, and knights are always coming to cut off my head. It's a perilous quest, you see, and knights like perilous quests. But I've got a cunning plan. Now we've been properly introduced I suppose I'd better show you.

(takes off his clawed hands)

Could you hold these? And can you help me with my head?

(**EMMA** *and* **LUCY** *help the* **JABBERWOCK** *take off his disguise, placing the various parts at the side of the stage.*)

LUCY. What a pity. You're quite ordinary looking without a disguise.

JABBERWOCK. That's why I wear it. How would knights be afraid of me looking like this?

EMMA. Why do you want knights to be afraid of you?

JABBERWOCK. So they won't cut off my head, of course.

EMMA. But if you didn't look frightening, they wouldn't *want* to cut your head off.

JABBERWOCK. I hadn't thought of that.

PERCY. That's all very well, but I've got a job to do. I'm going to cut your head off anyway.

JABBERWOCK. You can't do that! I'd die without a head. There'd be no more Jabberwock. I'm the only one in the world, you know. I don't want to become an extinct species.

PERCY. But I've got to take your head home to show my father.

JABBERWOCK. He'll want it on a silver platter, I suppose. They always want heads on silver platters.

PERCY. He'll want a golden one. He's very rich.

LUCY. *(aside)* What's a platter?

EMMA. *(aside)* It's a big plate. You put heads on them.

PERCY. Stand back. I'm going to cut his head right off.

LUCY. You can't!

(She stands in front of the **JABBERWOCK** *with her arms held out.)*

I won't let you.

PERCY. Out of my way – or I'll cut your head off too.

EMMA. You're not cutting her head off!

(She stands in front of **LUCY.** *)*

Anyway, that's only a toy sword. You couldn't possibly cut anybody's head off with that.

PERCY. When I had a real one I kept cutting people's fingers off, and things like that. They said I was a danger to man and beast. So they gave me this. Oh, this is hopeless! My father will be so disappointed. He wants me to be a hero.

LUCY. You can't go killing things just to be a hero. What about your vows of chivalry? Protecting the poor and the weak and the innocent?

PERCY. That's only damsons. It doesn't apply to dragons and wild beasts and things like that.

JABBERWOCK. I'm not a dragon or a wild beast – I'm a Jabberwock! The only one!

PERCY. I've still got to kill you. That's my job. I'm a knight.

EMMA. You're really a prince.

PERCY. How do you know?

EMMA. I met your mother. She's awfully worried about you.

PERCY. Is she? I didn't think she cared about me very much.

EMMA. Of course she cares. She wouldn't be looking for you if she didn't.

LUCY. Are you really a prince?

PERCY. Well, yes, but I'm a knight as well. I've got certificates and everything. Knights have all the fun. Going on perilous quests, saving damsons in distress, fighting dragons and such-like – princes just prance about.

EMMA. And fall in love with beautiful princesses.

PERCY. I've never met a beautiful princess. You're not a beautiful princess, by any chance?

EMMA. *(wistfully)* I'm afraid not.

LUCY. *(eagerly)* I could pretend to be one, if you like.

PERCY. It wouldn't be the same, I'm afraid.

LUCY. *(disappointed)* Oh.

EMMA. Why don't you want people to know you're a prince?

PERCY. Well, I'm a great disappointment to my father. Princes aren't allowed to be disappointments, so I thought if I didn't manage to cut the Jabberwock's head off it wouldn't be so bad if people thought I was only a knight.

EMMA. So you were just making things up, like Jim.

PERCY. But I really *am* a knight. He's just *pretending* to be a ferocious creature.

JABBERWOCK. I was using my imagination. Having thoughts.

EMMA. That means there must be a Tumtum Tree somewhere about.

(The **TUMTUM TREE** *enters.)*

TUMTUM TREE. Did somebody mention my name again?

EMMA. Well, I did, but it was only a passing thought again.

TUMTUM TREE. I thought so. But I'm only passing again. Tum tum. Again.

(The **TUMTUM TREE** *exits.)*

LUCY. But what about the jaws that bite, the claws that catch. Would you have eaten us?

JABBERWOCK. Of course not. I'm a herbivore. I only eat grass and things. I just wanted to scare you.

EMMA. What about all the knights who barely escaped with their lives?

JABBERWOCK. *(mysteriously)* Ah! Well!

(The light begins to fade.)

EMMA. You can't say 'Ah! Well!' in a mysterious manner and nothing else. It's very rude.

JABBERWOCK. It's all about imagination.

(lowering his voice and speaking mysteriously)

If you're in the middle of a wood and you hear strange noises, it's easy to think some fearsome creature is stalking you – and then your imagination really starts working…

(The light has continued to fade and it's now quite dark. The **FIRST BANDERSNATCH** *peers onstage downstage left and makes mysterious beckoning gestures.)*

EMMA. What's that? I thought I saw something. Over there.

(The **FIRST BANDERSNATCH** *disappears left.)*

JABBERWOCK. I told you. It's your imagination. You can imagine all sorts of things if you really try. You might even imagine the frumious Bandersnatch.

EMMA. Frumious? What's that?

JABBERWOCK. Well, its not usually spoken of in polite society.

(The **SECOND BANDERSNATCH** *peers on-stage upstage right and makes beckoning gestures.)*

LUCY. Look! There's that thing again.

PERCY. I see it. Over there.

(The **SECOND BANDERSNATCH** *disappears right.)*

EMMA. Oh, it's gone. What was it?

JABBERWOCK. *(in a low voice)* That was – the Bandersnatch.

PERCY. The Bandersnatch!

JABBERWOCK. Now the Bandersnatch is a real villain. The ones who never returned, the ones who never came galumphing back, the ones who were never seen again – the Bandersnatch got them.

(The **FIRST BANDERSNATCH** *peers on-stage upstage left and beckons.)*

PERCY. Look! Over there.

(The **FIRST BANDERSNATCH** *disappears left.)*

LUCY. It's gone. I wonder…

*(***LUCY** *begins to wander upstage left. The* **SECOND BANDERSNATCH** *peers on-stage downstage right and beckons.)*

PERCY. *(in a low voice)* Don't say anything, but there it is again.

(The **SECOND BANDERSNATCH** *disappears.)*

EMMA. What does it want?

PERCY. It's all right. It wouldn't dare try anything while I'm around.

(As **PERCY** *and* **EMMA** *start to move downstage right, the* **FIRST BANDERSNATCH** *appears upstage left, grabs* **LUCY** *and drags her off stage.* **LUCY** *gives a muffled cry.* **EMMA** *looks round – too late.)*

EMMA. Where's Lucy? She must've wandered off again. She's a most infuriating child!

JABBERWOCK. Oh dear. I rather think she might've been snatched.

PERCY. I'll have to rescue her, then. Come on Emma, you can watch the mighty hero in action.

*(**PERCY** draws his sword and exits upstage left.)*

JABBERWOCK. It's all right! It doesn't…

EMMA. Come on Jim, we have to rescue Lucy!

*(She exits upstage left. The **JABBERWOCK** reluctantly follows. The **SECOND BANDERSNATCH** enters right. **PERCY** enters downstage left.)*

PERCY. Hey there! Stand and fight!

*(The **SECOND BANDERSNATCH** exits right. **PERCY** follows. **EMMA** enters upstage center. The **FIRST BAND-ERSNATCH** enters left.)*

EMMA. Where's my sister? Stop!

*(The **FIRST BANDERSNATCH** exits left. **EMMA** follows. **PERCY** enters center as the **SECOND BANDERSNATCH** enters right.)*

PERCY. Come here! I want a word with you, manxsome creature!

*(The **SECOND BANDERSNATCH** exits right. **PERCY** follows. **EMMA** enters upstage center. **PERCY** enters right.)*

PERCY. Gadzooks and Oddsboddikins! Where's it gone?

EMMA. *(pointing off left)* It went that way.

*(The **SECOND BANDERSNATCH** enters right.)*

PERCY. *(pointing off right)* No! There it is!

*(The **SECOND BANDERSNATCH** exits Right.)*

EMMA. But I was sure it went that way, or perhaps there's –

*(The **FIRST BANDERSNATCH** enters left, sees them and exits left.)*

PERCY. Gadzooks and Oddsboddikins! How does it *do* that?

EMMA. There must be *two* of them!

PERCY. Two against one! Despicably unfair, but I'll take on both of them! Step forward, varlets! Have at thee!

(The **FIRST BANDERSNATCH** *enters downstage left and the* **SECOND BANDERSNATCH** *enters downstage right.* **PERCY** *brandishes his sword as they advance. The* **JABBERWOCK** *enters upstage center, and the* **BANDERSNATCHES** *step back from* **PERCY***. The light steadily increases during the following.)*

JABBERWOCK. Stop, Percy! Leave it to me.

(He confronts the **BANDERSNATCHES***.)*

You've done it again, haven't you? You've snatched someone.

FIRST BANDERSNATCH. No we haven't!

SECOND BANDERSNATCH. Well, perhaps.

FIRST BANDERSNATCH. Possibly.

SECOND BANDERSNATCH. Maybe.

FIRST BANDERSNATCH. All right. Yes.

SECOND BANDERSNATCH. But only a little one.

JABBERWOCK. Well, the little one's somebody's sister, and the sister wants her back.

PERCY. Hand her over, or I'll chop off your head.

JABBERWOCK. Stop it, Percy. There's no need for that.

PERCY. You must be joking! They've eaten Lucy!

FIRST BANDERSNATCH. *(horrified)* No we haven't! We couldn't eat anybody. We're vegetarians.

SECOND BANDERSNATCH. We haven't got her.

FIRST BANDERSNATCH. Well, we did, but she sort of got away. She tickled me! I'm awfully ticklish, you see, so I had to let her go.

(The **BOROGROVES** *enter with* **LUCY***.)*

SECOND BOROGROVE. Excuse me. We've found some lost property, and we think it might belong to you.

EMMA. It's my sister Lucy. I told you about her.

FIRST BOROGROVE. It's really too bad. You've done nothing but disrupt the smooth running of the wood since you came here, and now there's two of you. As large as life and three times as obvious. How on earth did you manage to lose her?

EMMA. I didn't *manage* it. I didn't mean to lose her in the first place.

FIRST BOROGROVE. Whether you meant to lose her in the first place, the second place or anyplace at all, we found her in this place, and if you take my advice you should lose her again as soon as possible. One of you is quite enough – two are impossible. You should throw her away. Put her in a rubbish bin.

LUCY. Nobody's going to put *me* in a rubbish bin!

EMMA. It's all right, Lucy. You're quite annoying sometimes, but I'm really very fond of you.

SECOND BOROGROVE. Ah. That explains everything. You'll have to keep her if you're fond of her.

FIRST BOROGROVE. That's all very well, but might I suggest that you both go home immediately and let Tulgey Wood return to its customary peaceful state. Good day!

(*The* **FIRST BOROGROVE** *exits.*)

SECOND BOROGROVE. I apologise most profusely for my friend's bad behaviour. By the way, if I might say, in complete confidence of course…

(*lowers his voice*)

You really shouldn't associate with Bandersnatches, you know. They're frightfully frumious.

LUCY. Frumious? What's that?

SECOND BOROGROVE. You'll find out soon enough, I'm afraid.

(*The* **SECOND BOROGROVE** *bows and exits.*)

LUCY. Why won't people tell me what frumious means?

(*sniffing.*)

What's that awful smell?

EMMA. I smelled it earlier, but I didn't like to say.

PERCY. I say! It isn't me is it? Mother's always telling me about personal hygiene.

FIRST BANDERSNATCH. I'm afraid it's us. We eat a lot of beans, you know. That's why people shun us. Sorry.

EMMA. So that's what frumious means!

SECOND BANDERSNATCH. Thinking of beans is making me hungry. It's supper time. We'd better go.

FIRST BANDERSNATCH. I'm sorry I snatched you. We wouldn't have hurt you. Honestly.

LUCY. That's all right.

SECOND BANDERSNATCH. If you hear any more stories about frumious Bandersnatches, just ignore them.

(The **BANDERSNATCHES** *exit.)*

JABBERWOCK. They're very shy, actually. You're lucky to have met them.

EMMA. We wouldn't have met them if they hadn't snatched Lucy!

LUCY. I'm all right. It was quite exciting, actually. And while I've been trying to find you I've been having uffish thoughts…

(The **TUMTUM TREE** *enters.)*

TUMTUM TREE. I know, I'm only passing. I'm always passing. I never get a chance to stay very long, and nobody ever listens to me. It's too too bad. Ah well, I suppose one must be philosophical about things. Such is life. Tum tum.

(The **TUMTUM TREE** *exits, still grumbling and tumtumming.)*

LUCY. I've thought of a cunning plan. All Percy has to do is go back and tell people how he braved dangers and disasters and fought the Jabberwock – and show them the Jabberwock's head!

JABBERWOCK. He's not cutting my head off!

LUCY. Your *disguise* head.

JABBERWOCK. My disguise head?

LUCY. *(picking up the disguise head)* Percy just has to pretend it's your real one.

PERCY. You mean – I'll have to lie?

LUCY. Let's just say you have to use your imagination.

PERCY. Well, I don't know.

EVERYBODY. Oh, go on!

PERCY. All right, if you insist.

EMMA. You'll make your mother and father so proud of you.

LUCY. And if everybody thinks it's the *real* Jabberwock's head, they won't bother coming to the wood to find him, will they? So Jim can live happily ever after.

EMMA. Lucy, that's brilliant!

LUCY. Yes it is, isn't it.

QUEEN. *(off)* Oh, our goodness! Oh, our beard and whiskers! Help! Somebody! Help!

JUBJUB BIRD. *(off)* Jubjub! Jubjub! Jubjub!

(The light fades dramatically as the **QUEEN** *enters right, pursued by the* **JUBJUB BIRD.** *She circles them without stopping, calling as she passes.)*

QUEEN. Percy! Our son! Help us! Help, help, help!

JUBJUB BIRD. Jubjub! Jubjub! Jubjub!

(The **QUEEN** *exits left, pursued by the* **JUBJUB BIRD.** *)*

PERCY. Gadzooks and Oddsboddikins! I must rescue her! Tallyho!

*(***PERCY** *exits left.)*

EMMA. We'd better help. Come on, Lucy.

(They exit left. The **JABBERWOCK** *stands aside, holding his false head, watching the following. The* **QUEEN** *enters right pursued by the* **JUBJUB BIRD,** *and they exit left.* **PERCY** *enters right and exits left.* **EMMA** *and* **LUCY** *enter right and exit left. The* **QUEEN** *enters right pursued by the* **JUBJUB BIRD,** *and they exit left.* **PERCY** *enters right and exits left.* **EMMA** *and* **LUCY** *enter right.)*

EMMA. Wait a minute. What are we doing? If we wait here they'll come to us!

LUCY. Are you sure?

EMMA. You'll see.

(The **QUEEN** *enters right and stops, exhausted. The* **JUBJUB BIRD** *enters right.)*

JUBJUB BIRD. Jubjub! Jubjub! Jubjub!

EMMA. We'll save you, your majesty. Get behind us.

(The **QUEEN** *scuttles behind* **EMMA** *and* **LUCY**, *who face the* **JUBJUB BIRD**. *The* **JABBERWOCK** *edges into the background.* **PERCY** *enters right.)*

PERCY. Stand back, Mother. Stand back, fair damsons! Have at thee, evil bird!

(The **JUBJUB BIRD** *turns.* **PERCY** *raises his sword and twirls it fantastically. The* **JUBJUB BIRD** *hesitates.)*

JUBJUB BIRD. That pointy thing hurts. I'm off!

(The **JUBJUB BIRD** *exits and normal lighting is restored.)*

QUEEN. Oh Percy! Our gallant son, facing ferocious monsters to save your mother and these fair damsels from a dreadful fate. How brave!

(The **QUEEN** *pats* **PERCY** *on the head, rather as if he's a dog.)*

PERCY. *(modestly but proudly)* Oh mother, it's nothing.

QUEEN. And you two. You two gels. Came to our aid. In the nick of time. Jolly good. Well done.

(The **QUEEN** *embraces* **EMMA** *and* **LUCY** *and then notices the* **JABBERWOCK** *standing aside. She's about to embrace him too, but has second thoughts.)*

JABBERWOCK. *(shyly)* Hello.

QUEEN. Haven't met you before. Who's this? Who's this?

JABBERWOCK. Me? Oh, I'm the Ja – just a nobody.

QUEEN. A nobody! Jolly good. Well done. What's that you're holding? Looks absolutely revolting!

JABBERWOCK. It's my – it's – it belongs to Percy.

(The **JABBERWOCK** *hands the fake head to* **LUCY** *who gives it to* **PERCY**.*)*

QUEEN. You own this disgusting object, Percy? How did you get it? Do hope you haven't been spending your pocket-money recklessly.

LUCY. *(whispering)* Go on. Tell her.

PERCY. Um – it's the Jabberwock's head, mother.

QUEEN. You've slain the Jabberwock!

PERCY. Well – yes, in a manner of speaking.

QUEEN. Callooh callay! Oh frabjous day! Come to our arms, our beamish boy!

(The QUEEN *embraces* PERCY, *who's embarrassed – but pleased.)*

PERCY. Mother! People are watching!

QUEEN. Must get used to being in the public eye, Percy. You're a celebrity now. We're so proud of you, we're chortling with joy! We must return to our palace. Say goodbye to your little friends, but don't delay. Callooh callay, oh frabjous day! Tally ho!

(The QUEEN *exits right, chortling, almost skipping with delight.)*

PERCY. Mother's proud of me! For the first time in my life she's actually proud of me. I don't know what to say.

EMMA. Don't say anything, go galumphing after her – quickly.

PERCY. Farewell, friends. You know, I've never had friends before.

LUCY. You have now. I know I'm not a beautiful princess, but – goodbye, Percy.

*(*LUCY *kisses* PERCY *on the cheek. He's astounded and delighted.)*

PERCY. Wow! It *is* a frabjous day!

(He exits right with the fake head. The JABBERWOCK *steps forward.)*

JABBERWOCK. Dear Lucy – and dear Emma, of course – I can't thank you enough.

LUCY. I'm pleased we could help.

EMMA. Now perhaps you can help us. How do we get out of this wood?

JABBERWOCK. Ah. Now. Well. It's just a matter of turning things round till you can see them properly. Beware the Jabberwock, you know.

LUCY. Not any more.

(She hugs the **JABBERWOCK.** *)*

I'm glad I met you, Jim. I'm going to miss you.

JABBERWOCK. Take care of yourself, Lucy. And take care of Emma too, of course. Goodbye.

(The **JABBERWOCK** *exits, turning and waving several times. The birds begin to sing.)*

EMMA. We ought to go home – before anything else happens. I wonder which way it is.

LUCY. *(thoughtfully)* He said 'Beware the Jabberwock', you know'…

(looks at the 'Beware the Jabberwock' sign)

'Sometimes it's just a matter of turning things round'…

(She turns the sign round to reveal a large painted arrow and the word 'Home'.)

You see! It's this way. Come on.

*(***LUCY** *takes* **EMMA***'s hand and they exit in the direction of the arrow as the light begins to fade. The* **TOVES** *flood onto the stage and then stop suddenly.)*

FIRST TOVE. The sun's gone.

SECOND TOVE. It's almost dark.

THIRD TOVE. We're too late.

ALL TOVES. Botheration!

(The light fades fast to blackout as the **TOVES** *exit sadly.)*

(curtain)

COSTUME

The characters provide a challenge for costume designers, who should let their imagination run riot. The original Tenniel illustrations for 'Jabberwocky' in 'Alice Through the Looking Glass' might provide inspiration, although of course they don't have to be followed. Effective four-legged creatures can be created by using disguised walking-sticks as the front 'legs'.

Toves look a little like scruffy badgers with lizard's feet and corkscrew noses.

Borogroves are shabby parrot-like birds with feathers sticking out all around, like live floor-mops.

Raths are a bit like small green pigs.

The Jubjub Bird has long legs *(stilts or platform shoes perhaps)* and a long pointed beak, which could be like a baseball cap with a very long peak.

The Jabberwock has a huge head, huge hands and feet with long claws, and a long tail. The head might be a ferocious mask with shining eyes worn as a large hat; the hands are large gloves with long claws, the feet are similar, while the tail can trail on the ground. Beneath his disguise, he should be wearing fantasy 'creature' makeup.

The Bandersnatch is very sneaky in everything it does. The two Bander-snatches wear identical creature masks, and should be impossible to tell apart. Extra-long fingers could be made from tubes of card.

Prince Percy takes big strides and tries to look gallant, but his sword is a toy one, and he wears a home-made loose outfit of rather shabby knitted chain-mail and a tattered surcoat. Perhaps the visor on his helmet could keep falling over his eyes at crucial moments.

FURNITURE AND PROPERTIES

On stage: Sundial
              Sign "Beware the Jabberwock!" with "Home" and an arrow on the reverse side
              Several signs "To Tulgey Wood" pointing in different directions
              Sign "Keep Off The Grass"
Personal: Book *(Emma)*
              Sword *(Percy)*

LIGHTING

Lighting should be used to create and enhance atmosphere, often fading up or down as imperceptibly as possible.

To open: *General lighting*
Cue 1:   Emma sleeps
    Cross-fade general lighting to woodland fantasy lighting
Cue 2:   Lucy: "Or is that the Jubjub Bird."
    Fade to dim as the Jubjub Bird crosses and then restore as Cue 1.
Cue 3:   Second Borogrove: "We ought to go, before – before it finds us."
    Fade to dim.
Cue 4:   Emma: "…before something nasty finds her!"
    Restore as Cue 1.
Cue 5:   Lucy: "And what about that Jubjub Bird?"
    Fade to dim as Jubjub Bird enters.
Cue 6:   The Jubjub Bird exits.
    Restore as Cue 1.
Cue 7:   Queen: "Come to your mother, Percy!" and exit.
    Fast fade to dim.
Cue 8:   Percy enters. Percy: "On guard!"
    Begin slow fade up to restore as Cue 1.
Cue 9:   Lucy: "One. Two. Three."
    Cue 8 fade up completed to restore as Cue 1.
Cue 10:   Jabberwock: "Ah! Well!"
    Begin fade to dim.
Cue 11:   Jabberwock: " – and then your imagination really starts working…"
    Cue 10 fade completed to dim.
Cue 12:   The Jabberwock enters
    Slow fade up to restore as Cue 1.
Cue 13:   The Queen enters pursued by the Jubjub Bird.
    Fade to dim.
Cue 14:   Jubjub Bird: "That pointy thing hurts. I'm off!"
    Restore as Cue 1.
Cue 15:   Jabberwock: "…take care of Emma too, of course. Goodbye." and exit
    Cross-fade to restore general lighting as at opening and begin fade.
Cue 16:   All Toves: "Botheration!"
    Fast fade to blackout – curtain.

EFFECTS

To open   *Woodland noises and birdsong. Fade out after entry of the Jubjub Bird.*
Cue 1:   Jabberwock: "…take care of Emma too, of course. Goodbye." and exit
    Fade up woodland noises and birdsong.

www.ingramcontent.com/pod-product-compliance
Lightning Source LLC
Chambersburg PA
CBHW061104050726
47592CB00004B/1819

* 9 7 8 0 8 7 4 4 0 2 1 5 5 *